ONE BEAR
IN
THE HOSPITAL

Caroline Bucknall

Dial Books for Young Readers · New York

To Nick

The bears were calling for a race.
Teddy planned to set the pace.

"Ready, Teddy?" said his friends.
"Let's race to where the pavement ends!"
"I am the fastest!" shouted Ted—
And clean forgot to look ahead.

He hit a rock! The careless bear
Was even faster through the air.
His friends all stopped to help poor Ted.
"We'll call an ambulance," they said.

They took him to the place that cares
For all the sick and injured bears.
"Where does it hurt, Ted? Here or there?"
Teddy told them, "Everywhere."

"This X ray shows us what to do
To make you feel as good as new.
Your broken leg will mend much faster
If we wrap it up in plaster."

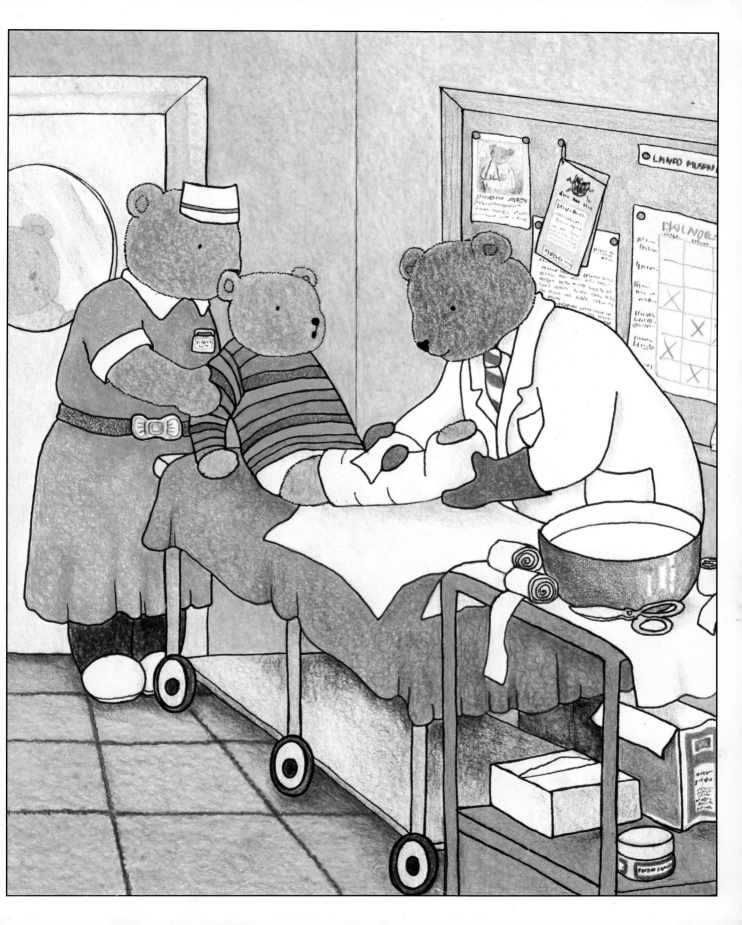

This hospital might make me well,
Thought Ted, but I don't like the smell.
When Mom came in the doctor said,
"He'll have to stay right here in bed."

Poor Teddy cried when Mom went home.
He couldn't sleep. He was alone.

"You'll soon feel better," smiled the nurse.
"I won't," said Teddy. "I'll feel worse."
Next morning lots of students came
To see him. "Gosh," said Teddy. "Fame!"

But lunch was not the sort of treat
A famous bear would want to eat.
"Poor Ted," said Nurse. "Try this dessert.
It's specially for bears that hurt."

The tasty pudding did the trick.
Thought Ted, Perhaps I'm not so sick.
He sorted through his box of toys
And talked to other girls and boys.

They came to sign his plaster cast.

When Ted made friends, the time soon passed.

The doctor saw the cheerful Ted.
"No need for you to stay in bed.
We're lending you a special chair
With wheels." "I like it!" cried the bear.

Mom asked the doctor, "Tell me when
Can I take my bear home again?"
The doctor smiled and said, "Today."
"I'm free at last," cried Ted. "Hooray!"

"Can I go out in my new chair?"
Asked Teddy. "Well," said Mom, "take care.
You've had a fright. It's pretty plain
You'll never want to race again!"

First published in the United States 1991
by Dial Books for Young Readers
A Division of Penguin Books USA Inc.
375 Hudson Street
New York, New York 10014
Published in Great Britain by Macmillan Children's Books
Copyright © 1990 by Caroline Bucknall
All rights reserved
Printed in Belgium
First Edition
N
1 3 5 7 9 10 8 6 4 2

Library of Congress Cataloging in Publication Data
Bucknall, Caroline.
One bear in the hospital / Caroline Bucknall.
p.   cm.
Summary: Ted Bear breaks his leg and undergoes
an overnight stay in the hospital.
ISBN 0-8037-0847-5
[1. Hospitals—Fiction. 2. Wounds and injuries—Fiction.
3. Bears—Fiction. 4. Stories in rhyme.] I. Title.
PZ8.3.B849One 1991   [E]—dc20   90-2994   CIP   AC